A Family of Poems

To Joss & Ali
Happy 3rd Birthday
Love, Grandma &
Grandpa
"06"

Caroline Kennedy

A Family of Poems

MY FAVORITE POETRY FOR CHILDREN

Paintings by JON J MUTH

HYPERION/HYPERION BOOKS FOR CHILDREN

New York

TABLE OF CONTENTS

Introduction by CAROLINE KENNEDY

ABOUT ME

THAT'S SO SILLY!

ANIMALS

THE SEASONS

THE SEASHORE

ADVENTURE

BEDTIME

INTRODUCTION

We live in a world of words and feelings that poems can help us understand. Poetry captures the most fleeting moments and makes them last forever, or describes the tiniest creature and makes it huge. Poets express our deepest emotions and ponder life's biggest questions in just a few lines that we can carry with us and bring to mind whenever we need them. Poems pass on the important values of love, faith, perseverance, and humor. They celebrate nature and the human spirit. We often turn to poetry at important moments in our lives because poets say exactly what we think and feel but can't find the words to describe. Just like our favorite songs, poems can be part of our everyday lives as well. They are funny; they inspire; they make us happy. Sharing a poem with a friend can start a conversation, change a mood, help us see things differently. Once we have read a poem a few times, it becomes part of us, just as the people we love and the times we share are part of us. I feel lucky to have poems as my lifelong companions.

Some people think poetry is solitary or boring. They worry that they won't be able to understand it. But people who start reading poems when they are young don't have these fears. As children, we enjoy exploring language and rhyme and creating word pictures of the world around us. A love of learning and the ability to express ourselves clearly are critical in today's world. We are bombarded with information, but growing up with poetry develops a foundation in language and values that enables us to distinguish what is truly important.

If our parents read to us as children, we remember the closeness of the moments together, the sound and power of voice and expression, the sense of wonder that a poem inspires, and the calm and safety of snuggling at bedtime. As we grow up and read those same poems with our own children, those memories will be unlocked and the poems carried forward by a new generation of readers.

Poetry played a special role in my family life. It brought the generations together and deepened our knowledge and feelings for one another. My grandmother recited "The Midnight Ride of Paul Revere" to teach us about American history, and her belief that each of us can change the world.

My mother began her lifelong relationship with literature by reading aloud with her grandfather, a turn-of-the-century gentleman-scholar with a handlebar mustache, whom she visited on Wednesday afternoons after dancing class. The first poem they memorized together was James Russell Lowell's "And What Is So Rare As a Day in June?" which is included in this book. One of her favorite lines appears at the beginning of the third stanza, "Now is the high-tide of the year," and that image was one that she applied to special times in life.

After her death, I collected and published *The Best-Loved Poems of Jacqueline Kennedy Onassis*. The most unexpected part of publishing that book was how many people spoke and wrote to me about sharing the same poems in their own families. They inspired me to work on this book for children and families who are starting to read and discover poetry. I have been fortunate to work with the gifted artist and author Jon J Muth, whose luminous watercolors enrich this book.

In our family, we were encouraged to write or choose a favorite poem for each holiday or birthday as a gift for my mother and grandparents instead of buying a card or present. My brother and I would copy over and illustrate our choices, and my mother pasted them in a special scrapbook. When I look through that poetry scrapbook today, it reminds me of our last-minute races to find the best poem, and it evokes who we were as well as if it were a photo album. Although John and I complained bitterly, we both secretly enjoyed our poetic explorations and the poems we collected later that became sources of both reflection and strength. My children have continued the tradition for me, including the complaining!

Many familiar favorites from our poetry scrapbook are in this collection, including "Sea-Fever" by John Masefield, "Who Has Seen the Wind?" by Christina Rossetti, and the Twenty-third Psalm. But we also chose less serious or well-known poems. One of my brother's particular favorites was "Careless Willie," about a boy who nails his sister to the door. I have no doubt that it was his older sister, and she probably looked a lot like me!

In recent years, poetry has enjoyed a resurgence. While in other countries poetry has long been a vibrant form of individual expression and social protest, after September 11, many Americans turned to poetry as a way of understanding and transforming their experiences. In addition, a generation of urban poets energized by rap and hip-hop has come of age using the spoken word to chronicle their lives and struggle. They have shown us that poetry is power—power to live your life fully and to realize your dreams. The younger we are when we start creating and articulating our experiences, the more easily we can find our path in life. The more we support children as they find their own voices, the farther they can go.

For the past few years I have been working in the New York City schools, where I have visited classes with students whose families come from around the world. One of the ways the teachers bring the children together is by asking them to read and write poems. As the children find their voices, they learn to listen more closely as well. My own experience and those visits gave me the title *A Family of Poems*, because those students have showed me how poetry can connect us to each other in new and powerful ways.

Caroline Kennedy
New York, 2005

Poetry has been called the language of the human heart, and part of what poems communicate can't even be put into words. But because poems speak an authentic language, they help us to teach as well as to learn. When we read a poem in which the poet is speaking from the heart, we can learn about ourselves as well as about the author, for poets put into words the feelings that all of us have.

As children, we believe the world revolves around us, and that sense of self has been perfectly expressed in poems of all kinds and complexity. Even simple poems like "The Early Morning" by Hilaire Belloc, or "First Fig" and "Second Fig" by Edna St. Vincent Millay help us think about who we are and how we fit into the world. When we get a little older, poems like "The Road Not Taken" by Robert Frost explore the choices we make, while the "Twenty-third Psalm" comforts us with the knowledge that God will protect us throughout our lives.

Writing poems can be hard because we want to choose the perfect words, yet can't always find them. It helps to know that great poets struggle too. William Butler Yeats, who wrote "The Lake Isle of Innisfree," rarely wrote more than seven lines a day, yet he is one of the greatest poets in the English language. Writing a poem forces us to think about what we really want to say, and helps us understand ourselves and shape our lives. If you start when you are young, you will see that words and ideas have the power to change the world.

ABOUT ME

THE EARLY MORNING

The moon on the one hand, the dawn on the other:
The moon is my sister, the dawn is my brother.
The moon on my left hand and the dawn on my right.
My brother, good morning: my sister, good night.

Hilaire Belloc

ME

As long as I live
I shall always be
My Self—and no other,
Just me.

Like a tree.
Willow, elder,
Aspen, thorn,
Or cypress forlorn.

Like a flower,
For its hour—
Primrose, or pink,
Or a violet—
Sunned by the sun,
And with dewdrops wet.

Always just me.

Walter de la Mare

FIRST FIG

My candle burns at both ends;
  It will not last the night;
But ah, my foes, and oh, my friends—
  It gives a lovely light!

Edna St. Vincent Millay

SECOND FIG

Safe upon the solid rock the ugly houses stand:
Come and see my shining palace built upon the sand!

Edna St. Vincent Millay

THIS IS JUST TO SAY

I have eaten
the plums
that were in
the icebox

and which
you were probably
saving
for breakfast

Forgive me
they were delicious
so sweet
and so cold

William Carlos Williams

TO P.J. (2 YRS. OLD WHO SED WRITE A POEM FOR ME IN PORTLAND, OREGON)

if i cud ever write a
poem as beautiful as u
little 2/yr/old/brotha,
i wud laugh, jump, leap
up and touch the stars
cuz u be the poem i try for
each time i pick up a pen and paper.
u. and Morani and Mungu
be our blue/blk/stars that
will shine on our lives and
makes us finally BE.
if i cud ever write a poem as beautiful
as u, little 2/yr/old/ brotha,
poetry wud go out of bizness.

Sonia Sanchez

16

THE REASON I LIKE
CHOCOLATE

The reason I like chocolate
is I can lick my fingers
and nobody tells me I'm not polite

I especially like scary movies
'cause I can snuggle with Mommy
or my big sister and they don't laugh

I like to cry sometimes 'cause
everybody says "what's the matter
don't cry"

and I like books
for all those reasons
but mostly 'cause they just make me
happy

and I really like
to be happy

Nikki Giovanni

17

MICHAEL IS AFRAID OF THE STORM

Lightning is angry in the night.
Thunder spanks our house.
Rain is hating our old elm—
It punishes the boughs.

Now, I am next to nine years old,
And crying's not for me.
But if I touch my mother's hand,
Perhaps no one will see.

And if I keep herself in sight—
Follow her busy dress—
No one will notice my wild eye.
No one will laugh, I guess.

Gwendolyn Brooks

18

"HOPE" IS THE THING WITH FEATHERS

"Hope" is the thing with feathers—
That perches in the soul—
And sings the tune without the words—
And never stops—at all—

And sweetest—in the Gale—is heard—
And sore must be the storm—
That could abash the little bird
That kept so many warm—

I've heard it in the chillest land—
And on the strangest Sea—
Yet, never, in Extremity,
It asked a crumb—of Me.

Emily Dickinson

I MAY, I MIGHT, I MUST

If you will tell me why the fen
appears impassable, I then
will tell you why I think that I
can get across it if I try.

Marianne Moore

19

THE LAKE ISLE OF INNISFREE

I will arise and go now, and go to Innisfree,
And a small cabin build there, of clay and wattles made:
Nine bean-rows will I have there, a hive for the honey-bee,
And live alone in the bee-loud glade.

And I shall have some peace there, for peace comes dropping slow,
Dropping from the veils of the morning to where the cricket sings;
There midnight's all a glimmer, and noon a purple glow,
And evening full of the linnet's wings.

I will arise and go now, for always night and day
I hear lake water lapping with low sounds by the shore;
While I stand on the roadway, or on the pavements grey,
I hear it in the deep heart's core.

William Butler Yeats

HAS MY HEART GONE TO SLEEP?

Has my heart gone to sleep?
Have the beehives of my dreams
stopped working, the waterwheel
of the mind run dry,
scoops turning empty,
only shadow inside?
   No, my heart is not asleep.
It is awake, wide awake.
Not asleep, not dreaming—
its eyes are opened wide
watching distant signals, listening
on the rim of the vast silence.

Antonio Machado
Translated by Alan S. Trueblood

21

THE ROAD NOT TAKEN

Two roads diverged in a yellow wood,
And sorry I could not travel both
And be one traveler, long I stood
And looked down one as far as I could
To where it bent in the undergrowth;

Then took the other, as just as fair,
And having perhaps the better claim,
Because it was grassy and wanted wear;
Though as for that the passing there
Had worn them really about the same,

And both that morning equally lay
In leaves no step had trodden black.
Oh, I kept the first for another day!
Yet knowing how way leads on to way,
I doubted if I should ever come back.

I shall be telling this with a sigh
Somewhere ages and ages hence:
Two roads diverged in a wood, and I—
I took the one less traveled by,
And that has made all the difference.

Robert Frost

PSALM 23: 1–6

A Psalm of David. The LORD is my shepherd; I shall not want.

He maketh me to lie down in green pastures: he leadeth me beside the still waters.

He restoreth my soul: he leadeth me in the paths of righteousness for his name's sake:

Yea, though I walk through the valley of the shadow of death, I will fear no evil: for thou art with me; thy rod and thy staff they comfort me.

Thou preparest a table before me in the presence of mine enemies: thou anointest my head with oil; my cup runneth over.

Surely goodness and mercy shall follow me all the days of my life: and I will dwell in the house of the LORD for ever.

Holy Bible, King James Version

These poems are for having fun. We all like to fool around, and playing with sounds and language is one of the first ways we explore our world. Silly poems are easy to collect and memorize—they remind us that things that seem funny can be serious underneath— and enjoying them encourages us to try reading different kinds of poems. Soon enough we realize that there is no poem we can't tackle, no idea we can't understand.

Serious poets write silly poems too. A. E. Housman, an influential English poet and Latin professor, wrote "Amelia Mixed the Mustard." The poem "Some Opposites" grew out of a game that poet laureate Richard Wilbur used to play with his children.

When you write your own poems you can be serious or lighthearted, you can make rhymes, you can arrange the words vertically or sideways, and you can express how you feel. In your poetry, you have the power to describe the world as it is, and as you want it to be. That is the first step to making it true.

THAT'S SO SILLY!

THERE WAS AN OLD MAN OF WEST DUMPET

There was an old man of West Dumpet,
Who possessed a large nose like a trumpet;
    When he blew it aloud,
    It astonished the crowd,
And was heard through the whole of
    West Dumpet.

Edward Lear

THERE WAS AN OLD MAN OF BLACKHEATH

There was an old man of Blackheath,
Who sat on his set of false teeth;
    Said he, with a start,
    "O Lord, bless my heart!
I've bitten myself underneath!"

Anonymous

THE LITTLE MAN WHO WASN'T THERE

As I was going up the stair
I met a man who wasn't there
He wasn't there again today
I wish, I wish he'd stay away.

William Hughes Mearns

MOSES

Moses supposes his toeses are roses,
But Moses supposes erroneously;
For nobody's toeses are posies of roses
As Moses supposes his toeses to be.

Anonymous

HAPPINESS

John had
Great Big
Waterproof
Boots on;
John had a
Great Big
Waterproof
Hat;
John had a
Great Big
Waterproof
Mackintosh—
And that
(Said John)
Is
That.

A. A. Milne

"AMELIA MIXED THE MUSTARD"

Amelia mixed the mustard,
    She mixed it good and thick;
She put it in the custard
    And made her Mother sick,
And showing satisfaction
    By many loud huzza
"Observe" said she "the action
    Of mustard on Mamma."

A. E. Housman

CARELESS WILLIE

Willie with a thirst for gore
Nailed his sister to the door
Mother said with humor quaint
"Careful, Willie, don't scratch the paint!"

Anonymous

TO A FELLOW POET

Sir, you are tough, and I am tough.
But who will write whose epitaph?

Joseph Brodsky

30

DADDY FELL INTO THE POND

Everyone grumbled. The sky was gray.
We had nothing to do and nothing to say.
We were nearing the end of a dismal day,
And there seemed to be nothing beyond,
                THEN
Daddy fell into the pond!

And everyone's face grew merry and bright,
And Timothy danced for sheer delight,
"Give me the camera, quick, oh quick!
He's crawling out of the duckweed." Click!

Then the gardener suddenly slapped his knee,
And doubled up, shaking silently,
And the ducks all quacked as if they were daft
And it sounded as if the old drake laughed.

O, there wasn't a thing that didn't respond
              WHEN
Daddy fell into the pond!

Alfred Noyes

THE PEOPLE UPSTAIRS

The people upstairs all practice ballet.
Their living room is a bowling alley.
Their bedroom is full of conducted tours.
Their radio is louder than yours.
They celebrate weekends all the week.
When they take a shower, your ceilings leak.
They try to get their parties to mix
By supplying their guests with Pogo sticks,
And when their orgy at last abates,
They go to the bathroom on roller skates.
I might love the people upstairs wondrous
If instead of above us, they just lived under us.

Ogden Nash

32

from Falling in Love Is Like Owning a Dog

AN EPITHALAMION

First of all, it's a big responsibility,
especially in a city like New York.
So think long and hard before deciding on love.
On the other hand, love gives you a sense of security:
when you're walking down the street late at night
and you have a leash on love
ain't no one going to mess with you.

Love doesn't like being left alone for long.
But come home and love is always happy to see you.
It may break a few things accidentally in its passion for life,
but you can never be mad at love for long.

Is love good all the time? No! No!
Love can be bad. Bad, love, bad! Very bad love.

Sometimes love just wants to go for a nice long walk.
It runs you around the block and leaves you panting.
It pulls you in several different directions at once,
or winds around and around you
until you're all wound up and can't move.

But love makes you meet people wherever you go.
People who have nothing in common but love
stop and talk to each other on the street.

Throw things away and love will bring them back,
again, and again, and again.
But most of all, love needs love, lots of it.
And in return, love loves you and never stops.

Taylor Mali

Today Is Very Boring

Today is very boring,
it's a very boring day,
there is nothing much to look at,
there is nothing much to say,
there's a peacock on my sneakers,
there's a penguin on my head,
there's a dormouse on my doorstep,
I am going back to bed.

Today is very boring,
it is boring through and through,
there is absolutely nothing
that I think I want to do,
I see giants riding rhinos,
and an ogre with a sword,
there's a dragon blowing smoke rings,
I am positively bored.

Today is very boring,
I can hardly help but yawn,
there's a flying saucer landing
in the middle of my lawn,
a volcano just erupted
less than half a mile away,
and I think I felt an earthquake,
it's a very boring day.

Jack Prelutsky

THE EMPEROR OF
ICE-CREAM

Call the roller of big cigars,
The muscular one, and bid him whip
In kitchen cups concupiscent curds.
Let the wenches dawdle in such dress
As they are used to wear, and let the boys
Bring flowers in last month's newspapers.
Let be be finale of seem.
The only emperor is the emperor of ice-cream.

Take from the dresser of deal,
Lacking the three glass knobs, that sheet
On which she embroidered fantails once
And spread it so as to cover her face.
If her horny feet protrude, they come
To show how cold she is, and dumb.
Let the lamp affix its beam.
The only emperor is the emperor of ice-cream.

Wallace Stevens

SOME OPPOSITES

The opposite of *standing still*
Is *walking up or down a hill*,
Running backwards, creeping, crawling,
Leaping off a cliff and falling,
Turning somersaults in gravel,
Or any other mode of travel.

The opposite of a *doughnut*? Wait
A minute while I meditate.
This isn't easy. Ah, I've found it!
A cookie with a hole around it.

What is the opposite of *two*?
A lonely me, a lonely you.

The opposite of a *cloud* could be
A white reflection in the sea,
Or *a huge blueness in the air,*
Caused by a cloud's not being there.

The opposite of *opposite*?
That's much too difficult. I quit.

Richard Wilbur

When I was young I had two kittens, two parakeets, a pony, a dog, and two hamsters whose babies got loose all over the White House. I was even given a Russian puppy whose mother had been the first dog in outer space. My cousins had an iguana, a giant tortoise, a monkey, and a red-tailed hawk who sat on our porch all summer because their house was too noisy.

These animals were my friends, and when I couldn't play with them, I had stuffed animals who came to life almost as convincingly. I used to line up the chairs in my room and sit my teddy bears down and read them stories and poems. They seemed to enjoy them very much.

The poems in this section are about all kinds of animals. Some poets write about animals they know well, like Ted Hughes does in "Roger the Dog." Others try to capture the essence of certain animals and the role they play in our lives. In Robert Frost's poem "The Last Word of a Bluebird," the friendly bluebird tells the little girl that spring will come again, whereas in Alfred, Lord Tennyson's "The Eagle," the bird is a majestic and terrifying predator. Poets remind us that animals have powers we admire: they are loving and cuddly, they help to feed and clothe us, they are strong and swift. These poems capture the qualities of many different animals and remind us to treasure wildness as well as companionship.

ANIMALS

Epigram: Engraved on the Collar of a Dog
Which I Gave to His Royal Highness

I am his Highness' dog at Kew;
Pray tell me, sir, whose dog are you?

Alexander Pope

Roger the Dog

Asleep he wheezes at his ease.
He only wakes to scratch his fleas.

He hogs the fire, he bakes his head
As if it were a loaf of bread.

He's just a sack of snoring dog,
You can lug him like a log.

You can roll him with your foot.
He'll stay snoring where he's put.

Take him out for exercise
He'll roll in cowclap up to his eyes.

He will not race, he will not romp.
He saves his strength for gobble and chomp.

He'll work as hard as you could wish
Emptying the dinner dish,

Then flops flat, and digs down deep,
Like a miner, into sleep.

Ted Hughes

THE SONG OF THE MISCHIEVOUS DOG

There are many who say that a dog has its day,
   And a cat has a number of lives;
There are others who think that a lobster is pink,
   And that bees never work in their hives.
There are fewer, of course, who insist that a horse
   Has a horn and two humps on its head,
And a fellow who jests that a mare can build nests
   Is as rare as a donkey that's red.
Yet in spite of all this, I have moments of bliss,
   For I cherish a passion for bones,
And though doubtful of biscuit, I'm willing to risk it,
   And I love to chase rabbits and stones.
But my greatest delight is to take a good bite
   At a calf that is plump and delicious;
And if I indulge in a bite at a bulge,
   Let's hope you won't think me too vicious.

Dylan Thomas

THE PORCUPINE

Any hound a porcupine nudges
Can't be blamed for harboring grudges.
I know one hound that laughed all winter
At a porcupine that sat on a splinter.

Ogden Nash

THE SLOTH

In moving-slow he has no Peer.
You ask him something in his Ear,
He thinks about it for a Year;

And, then, before he says a Word
There, upside down (unlike a Bird),
He will assume that you have Heard—

A most Ex-as-per-at-ing Lug.
But should you call his manner Smug,
He'll sigh and give his Branch a Hug;

Then off again to Sleep he goes,
Still swaying gently by his Toes,
And you just *know* he knows he knows.

Theodore Roethke

PEACOCKFEATHER

Peacockfeather:
peerless in your elegance,
how I loved you even as a child.
I took you for a love-token
which by silversilent ponds
elves in cool night hand each other,
when children all are gone to sleep.

And since good little Grandmama
often read me of wishing-wands,
I dreamed, you delicate of air,
there flowed in your fine filaments
the crafty force of the divining-rod—
and sought you in the summer grass.

Rainer Maria Rilke

ODE TO THE GOOSE

Goose, goose, goose,
You bend your neck towards the sky and sing.
Your white feathers float on the emerald water,
Your red feet push the clear waves.

Luo Binwang

MR. MISTOFFELEES

You ought to know Mr. Mistoffelees!
The Original Conjuring Cat—
(There can be no doubt about that).
Please listen to me and don't scoff. All his
Inventions are off his own bat.
There's no such Cat in the metropolis;
He holds all the patent monopolies
For performing surprising illusions
And creating eccentric confusions.
  At prestidigitation
    And at legerdemain
  He'll defy examination
    And deceive you again.
The greatest magicians have something to learn
From Mr. Mistoffelees' Conjuring Turn.
Presto!
    Away we go!
      And we all say: OH!
        Well I never!
          Was there ever
          A Cat so clever
            As Magical Mr. Mistoffelees!

He is quiet and small, he is black
From his ears to the tip of his tail;
He can creep through the tiniest crack
He can walk on the narrowest rail.
He can pick any card from a pack,
He is equally cunning with dice;
He is always deceiving you into believing
That he's only hunting for mice.
  He can play any trick with a cork

Or a spoon and a bit of fish-paste;
If you look for a knife or a fork
     And you think it is merely misplaced—
You have seen it one moment, and then it is *gawn*!
But you'll find it next week lying out on the lawn.
     And we all say: OH!
          Well I never!
          Was there ever
          A Cat so clever
               As Magical Mr. Mistoffelees!

His manner is vague and aloof,
You would think there was nobody shyer—
But his voice has been heard on the roof
When he was curled up by the fire.
And he's sometimes been heard by the fire
When he was about on the roof—
(At least we all *heard* that somebody purred)
Which is incontestable proof
     Of his singular magical powers:
          And I have known the family to call
          Him in from the garden for hours,
               While he was asleep in the hall.
And not long ago this phenomenal Cat
Produced *seven kittens* right out of a hat!
     And we all said: OH!
          Well I never!
          Did you ever
          Know a Cat so clever
               As Magical Mr. Mistoffelees!

                              T. S. Eliot

AN OLD SILENT POND

An old silent pond . . .
A frog jumps into the pond,
Splash! Silence again.

Basho

FAREWELL! LIKE A BEE

Farewell! Like a bee
reluctant to leave the deeps
of a peony.

Basho

THE FROG

Be kind and tender to the Frog,
   And do not call him names,
As "Slimy skin," or "Polly-wog,"
   Or likewise "Ugly James,"
Or "Gap-a-grin," or "Toad-gone-wrong,"
   Or "Billy Bandy-knees":

The frog is justly sensitive
   To epithets like these.
No animal will more repay
   A treatment kind and fair;
At least so lonely people say
   Who keep a frog (and, by the way,
They are extremely rare).

Hilaire Belloc

THE LITTLE TURTLE

There was a little turtle.
He lived in a box.
He swam in a puddle.
He climbed on the rocks.

He snapped at a mosquito.
He snapped at a flea.
He snapped at a minnow.
And he snapped at me.

He caught the mosquito.
He caught the flea.
He caught the minnow.
But he didn't catch me.

Vachel Lindsay

LITTLE TROTTY WAGTAIL

Little trotty wagtail he went in the rain,
And twittering, tottering sideways he ne'er got straight again.
He stooped to get a worm, and looked up to get a fly,
And then he flew away ere his feathers they were dry.

Little trotty wagtail, he waddled in the mud,
And left his little footmarks, trample where he would.
He waddled in the water-pudge, and waggle went his tail,
And chirrupt up his wings to dry upon the garden rail.

Little trotty wagtail, you nimble all about,
And in the dimpling water-pudge you waddle in and out;
Your home is nigh at hand, and in the warm pig-stye,
So, little Master Wagtail, I'll bid you a good-bye.

John Clare

"Hurt No Living Thing"

Hurt no living thing;
Ladybird, nor butterfly,
Nor moth with dusty wing,
Nor cricket chirping cheerily,
Nor grasshopper so light of leap,
Nor dancing gnat, nor beetle fat,
Nor harmless worms that creep.

Christina Rossetti

THE LAST WORD OF A BLUEBIRD
AS TOLD TO A CHILD

As I went out a Crow
In a low voice said, "Oh,
I was looking for you.
How do you do?
I just came to tell you
To tell Lesley (will you?)
That her little Bluebird
Wanted me to bring word
That the north wind last night
That made the stars bright
And made ice on the trough
Almost made him cough
His tail feathers off.
He just had to fly!
But he sent her Good-by,
And said to be good,
And wear her red hood,
And look for skunk tracks
In the snow with an ax—
And do everything!
And perhaps in the spring
He would come back and sing."

Robert Frost

51

SAINT FRANCIS AND THE SOW

The bud
stands for all things,
even for those things that don't flower,
for everything flowers, from within, of self-blessing;
though sometimes it is necessary
to reteach a thing its loveliness,
to put a hand on its brow
of the flower
and retell it in words and in touch
it is lovely
until it flowers again from within, of self-blessing;
as Saint Francis
put his hand on the creased forehead
of the sow, and told her in words and in touch
blessings of earth on the sow, and the sow
began remembering all down her thick length,
from the earthen snout all the way
through the fodder and slops to the spiritual curl
  of the tail,
from the hard spininess spiked out from the spine
down through the great broken heart
to the sheer blue milken dreaminess spurting
  and shuddering
from the fourteen teats into the fourteen mouths
  sucking and blowing beneath them:
the long, perfect loveliness of sow.

Galway Kinnell

THE CROCODILE

How doth the little crocodile
  Improve his shining tail,
And pour the waters of the Nile
  On every golden scale!

How cheerfully he seems to grin,
  How neatly spreads his claws,
And welcomes little fishes in,
  With gently smiling jaws!

Lewis Carroll

53

THE TYGER

Tyger! Tyger! burning bright
In the forests of the night,
What immortal hand or eye
Could frame thy fearful symmetry?

In what distant deeps or skies
Burnt the fire of thine eyes?
On what wings dare he aspire?
What the hand dare seize the fire?

And what shoulder, and what art,
Could twist the sinews of thy heart?
And when thy heart began to beat,
What dread hand? and what dread feet?

What the hammer? what the chain?
In what furnace was thy brain?
What the anvil? what dread grasp
Dare its deadly terrors clasp?

When the stars threw down their spears,
And water'd heaven with their tears,
Did he smile his work to see?
Did he who made the Lamb make thee?

Tyger! Tyger! burning bright
In the forests of the night,
What immortal hand or eye,
Dare frame thy fearful symmetry?

William Blake

HUNTING-SONG OF THE SEEONEE PACK

As the dawn was breaking the Sambhur belled
    Once, twice and again!
And a doe leaped up and a doe leaped up
From the pond in the wood where the wild deer sup.
This I, scouting alone, beheld,
    Once, twice and again!

As the dawn was breaking the Sambhur belled
    Once, twice and again!
And a wolf stole back, and a wolf stole back
To carry the word to the waiting pack,
And we sought and we found and we bayed on his track
    Once, twice and again!

As the dawn was breaking the Wolf Pack yelled
    Once, twice and again!
Feet in the jungle that leave no mark!
Eyes that can see in the dark—the dark!
Tongue—give tongue to it! Hark! O hark!
    Once, twice and again!

Rudyard Kipling

BUFFALO DUSK

The buffaloes are gone.
And those who saw the buffaloes are gone.
Those who saw the buffaloes by thousands and how they
　　pawed the prairie sod into dust with their hoofs, their
　　great heads down pawing on in a great pageant of dusk,
Those who saw the buffaloes are gone.
And the buffaloes are gone.

Carl Sandburg

ELEPHANT

Elephant, a spirit in the bush,
Elephant who brings death.
He swallows a whole palmfruit
thorns and all.
He tramples down the grass
with his mortar legs.
Wherever he walks
the grass is forbidden to stand up again.
He tears a man like an old rag
and hangs him up in the tree.
With his single hand
he pulls two palm trees to the ground.
If he had two hands
he would tear the heaven to shreds.
An elephant is not a load for an old man—
nor for a young man either.

Anonymous
From the Yoruba

58

THE EAGLE

He clasps the crag with crooked hands;
Close to the sun in lonely hands,
Ringed with the azure world, he stands.

The wrinkled sea beneath him crawls;
He watches from his mountain walls,
And like a thunderbolt he falls.

Alfred, Lord Tennyson

The world around us is always changing in ways we may not notice from day to day, but poems capture these tiny changes and special celebrations in the natural world—daffodils waving in the wind, geese honking overhead in the gray autumn sky, or snow covering everything white. Some changes happen almost invisibly—one day the light seems different, the days are longer, and there is time to go outside after school. The great Spanish poet Antonio Machado wrote about this transformation:

> *Spring has come*
> *Nobody knows how it happened.*

Poetry connects the different times of year with our deepest emotions—joy, sadness, faith, and love. The passage from the Book of Ecclesiastes and the Iroquois prayer share an acceptance of our place in the natural world. Shakespeare's sonnet "Shall I Compare Thee to a Summer's Day?" connects the woman he loves to one of God's most beautiful creations, and in "Who Has Seen the Wind?" Christina Rossetti reminds us that some of the most powerful forces in our lives are not visible.

At some point in our school years, we all have to write a poem about autumn. I always liked my mother's poem "Thoughts," because it captures the feeling of sitting in school daydreaming about a life of adventure. I include it here to inspire future poets during those back-to-school days.

THE SEASONS

ECCLESIASTES 3:1–8

To every thing there is a season, and a time to every purpose under the heaven:
A time to be born, and a time to die;
a time to plant,
and a time to pluck up that which is planted;
A time to kill, and a time to heal;
a time to break down, and a time to build up;
A time to weep, and a time to laugh;
a time to mourn, and a time to dance;
A time to cast away stones, and a time to gather stones together;
a time to embrace, and a time to refrain from embracing;
A time to seek, and a time to lose;
a time to keep, and a time to cast away;
A time to rend, and a time to sew;
a time to keep silence, and a time to speak;
A time to love, and time to hate;
a time for war, and a time for peace.

Holy Bible, King James Version

APRIL RAIN SONG

Let the rain kiss you.
Let the rain beat upon your head with silver liquid drops.
Let the rain sing you a lullaby.

The rain makes still pools on the sidewalk.
The rain makes running pools in the gutter.
The rain plays a little sleep-song on our roof at night—

And I love the rain.

Langston Hughes

IN JUST-

in Just-
spring   when the world is mud-
luscious the little
lame balloonman

whistles   far   and wee

and eddieandbill come
running from marbles and
piracies and it's
spring

when the world is puddle-wonderful

the queer
old balloonman whistles
far   and   wee
and bettyandisbel come dancing

from hop-scotch and jump-rope and

it's
spring
and
    the

        goat-footed

balloonMan   whistles
far
and
wee

e. e. cummings

65

PIPPA'S SONG

The year's at the spring
And day's at the morn;
Morning's at seven;
The hillside's dew-pearled;
The lark's on the wing;
The snail's on the thorn:
God's in his heaven—
All's right with the world!

Robert Browning

THE PASTURE

I'm going out to clean the pasture spring;
I'll only stop to rake the leaves away
(And wait to watch the water clear, I may):
I sha'n't be gone long.—You come too.

I'm going out to fetch the little calf
That's standing by the mother. It's so young,
It totters when she licks it with her tongue.
I sha'n't be gone long.—You come too.

Robert Frost

THE DAFFODILS

I wandered lonely as a cloud
That floats on high o'er vales and hills,
When all at once I saw a crowd,
A host, of golden daffodils;
Beside the lake, beneath the trees,
Fluttering and dancing in the breeze.

Continuous as the stars that shine
And twinkle on the milky way,
They stretched in never-ending line
Along the margin of a bay:
Ten thousand saw I at a glance,
Tossing their heads in sprightly dance.

The waves beside them danced; but they
Outdid the sparkling waves in glee:
A poet could not be but gay,
In such a jocund company:
I gazed—and gazed—but little thought
What wealth the show to me had brought:

For oft, when on my couch I lie
In vacant or in pensive mood,
They flash upon that inward eye
Which is the bliss of solitude;
And then my heart with pleasure fills,
And dances with the daffodils.

William Wordsworth

ARIEL'S SONG
The Tempest V, i, 104–110

Where the bee sucks, there suck I:
In a cowslip's bell I lie;
There I couch when owls do cry.
On the bat's back I do fly
After summer merrily:
  Merrily, merrily, shall I live now,
  Under the blossom that hangs on the bough.

William Shakespeare

THE ROSE FAMILY

The rose is a rose,
And was always a rose.
But the theory now goes
That the apple's a rose,
And the pear is, and so's
The plum, I suppose.
The dear only knows
What will next prove a rose.
You, of course, are a rose—
But were always a rose.

Robert Frost

"And What Is So Rare As a Day in June?"

And what is so rare as a day in June?
   Then, if ever, come perfect days;
Then Heaven tries the earth if it be in tune,
   And over it softly her warm ear lays:
Whether we look, or whether we listen,
We hear life murmur, or see it glisten;
Every clod feels a stir of might,
   An instinct within it that reaches and towers,
And, groping blindly above it for light,
   Climbs to a soul in grass and flowers;
The flush of life may well be seen
   Thrilling back over hills and valleys;
The cowslip startles in meadows green,
The buttercup catches the sun in its chalice,
And there's never a leaf nor a blade too mean
   To be some happy creature's palace;
The little bird sits at his door in the sun,
   Atilt like a blossom among the leaves,
And lets his illumined being o'errun
   With the deluge of summer it receives;

His mate feels the eggs beneath her wings,
And the heart in her dumb breast flutters and sings;
He sings to the wide world, and she to her nest,—
In the nice ear of Nature which song is the best?

Now is the high-tide of the year,
   And whatever of life hath ebbed away
Comes flooding back with a ripply cheer,
   Into every bare inlet and creek and bay;
Now the heart is so full that a drop overfills it,
We are happy now because God wills it;

No matter how barren the past may have been,
'Tis enough for us now that the leaves are green;
We sit in the warm shade and feel right well
How the sap creeps up and the blossoms swell;
We may shut our eyes but we cannot help knowing
That skies are clear and grass is growing;
The breeze comes whispering in our ear,
That dandelions are blossoming near,
   That maize has sprouted, that streams are flowing,
That the river is bluer than the sky,
That the robin is plastering his house hard by;
And if the breeze kept the good news back,
For our couriers we should not lack;
   We could guess it all by yon heifer's lowing,
And hark! How clear bold chanticleer,
Warmed with the new wine of the year,
   Tells all in his lusty crowing!

Joy comes, grief goes, we know not how;
Everything is happy now,
   Everything is upward striving;
'Tis as easy now for the heart to be true
As for grass to be green or skies to be blue,
   'Tis for the natural way of living:
Who knows whither the clouds have fled?
   In the unscarred heaven they leave not wake,
And the eyes forget the tears they have shed,
   The heart forgets its sorrow and ache;
The soul partakes the season's youth,
   And the sulphurous rifts of passion and woe
Lie deep 'neath a silence pure and smooth,
   Like burnt-out craters healed with snow.

                              James Russell Lowell

Sonnet XVIII
"Shall I Compare Thee to a Summer's Day?"

Shall I compare thee to a summer's day?
Thou art more lovely and more temperate:
Rough winds do shake the darling buds of May,
And summer's lease hath all too short a date:
Sometime too hot the eye of heaven shines,
And often is his gold complexion dimm'd:
And every fair from fair sometime declines,
By chance, or nature's changing course untrimm'd;
But thy eternal summer shall not fade,
Nor lose possession of that fair thou ow'st,
Nor shall death brag thou wand'rest in his shade,
When in eternal lines to time thou grow'st;
    So long as men can breathe, or eyes can see,
    So long lives this, and this gives life to thee.

William Shakespeare

Who Has Seen the Wind?

Who has seen the wind?
Neither I nor you:
But when the leaves hang trembling,
The wind is passing through.

Who has seen the wind?
Neither you nor I:
But when the trees bow down their heads,
The wind is passing by.

Christina Rossetti

THESE ARE THE DAYS WHEN BIRDS COME BACK

These are the days when Birds come back—
A very few—a Bird or two—
To take a backward look.

These are the days when skies resume
The old—old sophistries of June—
A blue and gold mistake.

Oh fraud that cannot cheat the Bee—
Almost thy plausibility
Induces my belief.

Till ranks of seeds their witness bear—
And softly thro' the altered air
Hurries a timid leaf.

Oh, Sacrament of summer days,
Oh, Last Communion in the Haze—
Permit a child to join,

Thy sacred emblems to partake—
Thy consecrated bread to break,
And thine immortal wine!

Emily Dickinson

THOUGHTS

I love the Autumn,
And yet I cannot say
All the thoughts and things
That make me feel this way.

I love walking on the angry shore,
To watch the angry sea;
Where summer people were before,
But now there's only me.

I love wood fires at night
That have a ruddy glow.
I stare at the flames
And think of long ago.

I love the feeling down inside me
That says to run away
To come and be a gypsy
And laugh the gypsy way.

The tangy taste of apples,
The snowy mist at morn,
The wanderlust inside you
When you hear the huntsman's horn.

Nostalgia—that's the Autumn,
Dreaming through September
Just a million lovely things
I always will remember.

Jacqueline Bouvier

SOMETHING TOLD THE WILD GEESE

Something told the wild geese
  It was time to go.
Though the fields lay golden
  Something whispered,—"Snow."
Leaves were green and stirring,
  Berries, luster-glossed,
But beneath warm feathers
  Something cautioned,—"Frost."
All the sagging orchards
  Steamed with amber spice,
But each wild breast stiffened
  At remembered ice.
Something told the wild geese
  It was time to fly,—
Summer sun was on their wings,
  Winter in their cry.

Rachel Field

FROM ODE TO A PAIR OF SOCKS

Maru Mori brought me
a pair
of socks
that she knit with her
shepherd's hands.
Two socks as soft
as rabbit fur.
I thrust my feet
inside them
as if they were
two
little boxes
knit
from threads
of sunset
and sheepskin.

My feet were
two woolen
fish
in those outrageous socks,
two gangly,
navy-blue sharks
impaled

on a golden thread,
two giant blackbirds,
two cannons:
thus
were my feet
honored
by
those
heavenly
socks.
They were
so beautiful
I found my feet
unlovable
for the very first time,
like two crusty old
firemen, firemen
unworthy
of that embroidered
fire,
those incandescent
socks.

Pablo Neruda

81

Snow in the Suburbs

Every branch big with it,
Bent every twig with it;
Every fork like a white web-foot;
Every street and pavement mute:
Some flakes have lost their way, and grope back upward when
Meeting those meandering down they turn and descend again.
The palings are glued together like a wall,
And there is no waft of wind with the fleecy fall.

A sparrow enters the tree,
Whereon immediately
A snow-lump thrice his own slight size
Descends on him and showers his head and eyes,
And overturns him,
And near inurns him,
And lights on a nether twig, when its brush
Starts off a volley of other lodging lumps with a rush.

The steps are a blanched slope,
Up which, with feeble hope,
A black cat comes, wide-eyed and thin;
And we take him in.

Thomas Hardy

STOPPING BY WOODS ON A SNOWY EVENING

Whose woods these are I think I know.
His house is in the village though;
He will not see me stopping here
To watch his woods fill up with snow.

My little horse must think it queer
To stop without a farmhouse near
Between the woods and frozen lake
The darkest evening of the year.

He gives his harness bells a shake
To ask if there is some mistake.
The only other sound's the sweep
Of easy wind and downy flake.

The woods are lovely, dark and deep.
But I have promises to keep,
And miles to go before I sleep,
And miles to go before I sleep.

Robert Frost

A Visit from St. Nicholas

'Twas the night before Christmas, when all through the house
Not a creature was stirring, not even a mouse;
The stockings were hung by the chimney with care,
In hopes that St. Nicholas soon would be there;
The children were nestled all snug in their beds,
While visions of sugar-plums danced in their heads;
And mamma in her kerchief, and I in my cap,
Had just settled down for a long winter's nap,—
When out on the lawn there arose such a clatter,
I sprang from the bed to see what was the matter.
Away to the window I flew like a flash,
Tore open the shutters and threw up the sash.
The moon on the breast of the new-fallen snow
Gave the lustre of midday to objects below;
When what to my wondering eyes should appear,
But a miniature sleigh and eight tiny reindeer,
With a little old driver, so lively and quick
I knew in a moment it must be St. Nick.
More rapid than eagles his coursers they came,
And he whistled and shouted, and called them by name:
"Now, Dasher! now, Dancer! now, Prancer and Vixen!
On, Comet! on, Cupid! on, Donder and Blitzen!
To the top of the porch! to the top of the wall!
Now dash away! dash away! dash away all!"
As dry leaves that before the wild hurricane fly,
When they meet with an obstacle, mount to the sky,

So up to the house-top the coursers they flew,
With the sleigh full of toys,—and St. Nicholas too.
And then, in a twinkling I heard on the roof
The prancing and pawing of each little hoof.
As I drew in my hand, and was turning around,
Down the chimney St. Nicholas came with a bound.
He was dressed all in fur from his head to his foot,
And his clothes were all tarnished with ashes and soot;
A bundle of toys he had flung on his back,
And he looked like a peddler just opening his pack.
His eyes, how they twinkled! his dimples, how merry!
His cheeks were like roses, his nose like a cherry;
His droll little mouth was drawn up like a bow,
And the beard of his chin was as white as the snow.
The stump of a pipe he held tight in his teeth,
And the smoke it encircled his head like a wreath.
He had a broad face and a little round belly
That shook, when he laughed, like a bowl full of jelly.
He was chubby and plump,—a right jolly old elf;
And I laughed, when I saw him, in spite of myself,
A wink of his eye and a twist of his head
Soon gave me to know I had nothing to dread.
He spoke not a word, but went straight to his work,
And filled all the stockings; then turned with a jerk,
And laying his finger aside of his nose,
And giving a nod, up the chimney he rose.
He sprang to his sleigh, to his team gave a whistle,
And away they all flew like the down of a thistle;
But I heard him exclaim, ere he drove out of sight,
"Happy Christmas to all, and to all a good-night!"

Clement Clarke Moore

87

LITTLE TREE

little tree
little silent Christmas tree
you are so little
you are more like a flower

who found you in the green forest
and were you very sorry to come away?
see   i will comfort you
because you smell so sweetly

i will kiss your cool bark
and hug you safe and tight
just as your mother would,
only don't be afraid

look   the spangles
that sleep all the year in a dark box
dreaming of being taken out and allowed to shine,
the balls the chains red and gold the fluffy threads,

put up your little arms
and i'll give them all to you to hold
every finger shall have its ring
and there won't be a single place dark or unhappy

then when you're quite dressed
you'll stand in the window for everyone to see
and how they'll stare!
oh but you'll be very proud

and my little sister and i will take hands
and looking up at our beautiful tree
we'll dance and sing
"Noel Noel"

e. e. cummings

IROQUOIS PRAYER

We return thanks to our mother, the earth,
   which sustains us.
We return thanks to the rivers and streams,
   which supply us with water.
We return thanks to all herbs, which furnish
   medicines for the care of our diseases.
We return thanks to the corn, and to her sisters,
   the beans and squashes, which give us life.
We return thanks to the bushes and trees,
   which provide us with fruit.
We return thanks to the wind,
   which, moving the air, has banished diseases.
We return thanks to the moon and stars,
   which have given us their light when the sun was gone.
We return thanks to our grandfather Hé-no,
   that he has protected his grandchildren from
   witches and reptiles, and has given to us his rain.
We return thanks to the sun, that has looked upon
   the earth with a beneficent eye.
Lastly, we return thanks to the Great Spirit,
   in whom is embodied all goodness, and who
   directs all things for the good of his children.

Anonymous

Everyone has places that are special to them. Some people like to be in the woods, or mountains, or out in the city at night. In my family, our special place is by the sea. As children, we built sand castles and collected hermit crabs together, competed in swimming races and went on sailing picnics. As we grew older we prepared for hurricanes or walked on the beach after a storm. These shared experiences gave our family a sense of closeness, a lot of fun and laughter, and a common outlook on life.

For all these reasons, poems about the sea are my favorites. In "maggie and milly and molly and may," E. E. Cummings captures the excitement of exploring the beach on a summer afternoon and the feeling that you've traveled to another world when you come home for dinner. Spending time by the ocean can also spark a love of history, a desire to explore the world, and a curiosity about the creatures that live beneath the waves. When summer is over and we go back to school, reading poems and stories can help us keep that spirit alive. John Masefield's poem "Sea-Fever," which begins with the line "I must go down to the seas again," calls us to a life of adventure no matter what time of year we read it.

Whether your special place is in your own backyard, or somewhere you visit with your family, through sound and images poems capture special wishes and memories. Reading and reciting the poems later brings those thoughts back to life even if you haven't left your own room.

THE SEASHORE

SEA JOY

When I go down by the sandy shore
I can think of nothing I want more
Than to live by the booming blue sea
As the seagulls flutter round about me

I can run about—when the tide is out
With the wind and the sand and the sea all about
And the seagulls are swirling and diving for fish
Oh—to live by the sea is my only wish.

Jacqueline Bouvier

MAGGIE AND MILLY AND MOLLY AND MAY

maggie and milly and molly and may
went down to the beach(to play one day)

and maggie discovered a shell that sang
so sweetly she couldn't remember her troubles,and

milly befriended a stranded star
whose rays five languid fingers were;

and molly was chased by a horrible thing
which raced sideways while blowing bubbles:and

may came home with a smooth round stone
as small as a world and as large as alone.

For whatever we lose(like a you or a me)
it's always ourselves we find in the sea

e. e. cummings

SEA SHELL

Sea Shell, Sea Shell,
Sing me a song, please!
A song of ships, and sailormen,
And parrots, and tropical trees,
Of islands lost in the Spanish Main,
Which no man ever may find again,
Of fishes and corals under the waves,
And seahorses stabled in great green caves.

Sea Shell, Sea Shell,
Sing of the things you know so well.

Amy Lowell

"FULL FATHOM FIVE"
The Tempest I, i, 398–405

Full fathom five thy father lies,
  Of his bones are coral made,
Those are pearls that were his eyes:
  Nothing of him that doth fade
But doth suffer a sea-change
Into something rich and strange.
Sea-nymphs hourly ring his knell.
Hark! now I hear them: ding, dong, bell!

William Shakespeare

THE OCTOPUS

Tell me, O Octopus, I begs,
Is those things arms, or is they legs?
I marvel at thee, Octopus;
If I were thou, I'd call me Us.

Ogden Nash

THE MOCK TURTLE'S SONG

"Will you walk a little faster?" said a whiting to a snail,
"There's a porpoise close behind us, and he's treading on my tail.
See how eagerly the lobsters and the turtles all advance?
They are waiting on the shingle—will you come and join the dance?
Will you, won't you, will you, won't you, will you join the dance?
Will you, won't you, will you, won't you, won't you join the dance?

"You can really have no notion how delightful it will be,
When they take us up and throw us, with the lobsters, out to sea!"
But the snail replied, "Too far, too far!" and gave a look askance—
Said he thanked the whiting kindly, but he would not join the dance.
Would not, could not, would not, could not, would not join the dance.
Would not, could not, would not, could not, could not join the dance.

"What matters it how far we go?" his scaly friend replied,
"There is another shore, you know, upon the other side.
The further off from England the nearer is to France—
Then turn not pale, beloved snail, but come and join the dance.
Will you, won't you, will you, won't you, will you join the dance?
Will you, won't you, will you, won't you, won't you join the dance?"

Lewis Carroll

A JELLY-FISH

Visible, invisible,
a fluctuating charm
an amber-tinctured amethyst
inhabits it, your arm
approaches and it opens
and it closes; you had meant
to catch it and it quivers;
you abandon your intent.

Marianne Moore

SEASHELL
To Natalia Jiménez

Someone brought me a seashell.

Singing inside
is a sea from a map.
My heart
fills up with water
and little tiny fish,
silvery, shadowy.

Someone brought me a seashell.

Federico García Lorca

THE FISH

I caught a tremendous fish
and held him beside the boat
half out of water, with my hook
fast in a corner of his mouth.
He didn't fight.
He hadn't fought at all.
He hung a grunting weight,
battered and venerable
and homely. Here and there
his brown skin hung in strips
like ancient wallpaper,
and its pattern of darker brown
was like wallpaper:
shapes like full-blown roses
stained and lost through age.
He was speckled with barnacles,
fine rosettes of lime,
and infested
with tiny white sea-lice,

and underneath two or three
rags of green weed hung down.
While his gills were breathing in
the terrible oxygen
—the frightening gills,
fresh and crisp with blood,
that can cut so badly—
I thought of the coarse white flesh
packed in like feathers,
the big bones and the little bones,
the dramatic reds and blacks
of his shiny entrails,
and the pink swim-bladder
like a big peony.
I looked into his eyes
which were far larger than mine
but shallower, and yellowed,
the irises backed and packed
with tarnished tinfoil

seen through the lenses
of old scratched isinglass.
They shifted a little, but not
to return my stare.
—It was more like the tipping
of an object toward the light.
I admired his sullen face,
the mechanism of his jaw,
and then I saw
that from his lower lip
—if you could call it a lip—
grim, wet, and weaponlike,
hung five old pieces of fish-line,
or four and a wire leader
with the swivel still attached,
with all their five big hooks
grown firmly in his mouth.
A green line, frayed at the end
where he broke it, two heavier lines,
and a fine black thread
still crimped from the strain and snap

when it broke and he got away.
Like medals with their ribbons
frayed and wavering,
a five-haired beard of wisdom
trailing from his aching jaw.
I stared and stared
and victory filled up
the little rented boat,
from the pool of bilge
where oil had spread a rainbow
around the rusted engine
to the bailer rusted orange,
the sun-cracked thwarts,
the oarlocks on their strings,
the gunnels—until everything
was rainbow, rainbow, rainbow!
And I let the fish go.

Elizabeth Bishop

SEA-FEVER

I must go down to the seas again, to the lonely sea and the sky,
And all I ask is a tall ship and a star to steer her by,
And the wheel's kick and the wind's song and the white sail's shaking
And a grey mist on the sea's face and a grey dawn breaking.

I must down to the seas again, for the call of the running tide
Is a wild call and a clear call that may not be denied;
And all I ask is a windy day with the white clouds flying,
And the flung spray and the blown spume, and the sea-gulls crying.

I must down to the seas again to the vagrant gypsy life,
To the gull's way and the whale's way where the wind's like a whetted knife;
And all I ask is a merry yarn from a laughing fellow-rover,
And quiet sleep and a sweet dream when the long trick's over.

John Masefield

101

Poems describe all kinds of adventures. Some are imaginary escapades, some tell of faraway places, while other journeys take place close to home. Poems about adventures help us to try new things, explore new places, and create new worlds.

Two of my favorite poems are "The Owl and the Pussycat" by Edward Lear and "The Song of Wandering Aengus" by W. B. Yeats. I still remember imagining the voyage of the "beautiful pea-green boat" while my mother read to me of the "land where the bong-tree grows." In Yeats's poem, the adventure begins with a walk to the hazel wood and becomes a lifelong journey between this world and a mythic one. When I first memorized it for a school poetry contest, I thought its images mystical and strange, and though they have become more familiar over the years, they are no less magical.

Not all adventures involve physical journeys—some poets write about changes within ourselves or between us and our friends. "Good Hotdogs" by Sandra Cisneros is about having lunch with a best friend. In "Scaffolding," Seamus Heaney describes the strength of a relationship built over many years. Other poems inspire us to try things we might be afraid of. Gwendolyn Brooks, the first African American writer to win a Pulitzer Prize, wrote about prejudice and the struggle for civil rights. Her poem "do not be afraid of no" challenges us with the words "It is brave to be involved."

ADVENTURE

THE SWING

How do you like to go up in a swing,
    Up in the air so blue?
"Oh, I do think it the pleasantest thing
    Ever a child can do!"

"Up in the air and over the wall,
    Till I can see so wide,
Rivers and trees and cattle and all
    Over the countryside—

"Till I look down on the garden green
    Down on the roof so brown—
Up in the air I go flying again,
    Up in the air and down!"

Robert Louis Stevenson

THIS IS THE KEY

This is the key of the kingdom:
In that kingdom there is a city.
In that city there is a town.
In that town there is a street.
In that street there is a lane.
In that lane there is a yard.
In that yard there is a house.
In that house there is a room.
In that room there is a bed.
On that bed there is a basket.
In that basket there are some flowers.
Flowers in a basket.
Basket on the bed.
Bed in the room.
Room in the house.
House in the yard.
Yard in the lane.
Lane in the street.
Street in the town.
Town in the city.
City in the kingdom.
Of the kingdom this is the key.

Anonymous

A FAIRY IN ARMOR

He put his acorn helmet on;
It was plumed of the silk of the thistle down;
The corslet plate that guarded his breast
Was once the wild bee's golden vest;
His cloak, of a thousand mingled dyes,
Was formed of the wings of butterflies;
His shield was the shell of a lady-bug green,
Studs of gold on a ground of green;
And the quivering lance which he brandished bright,
Was the sting of a wasp he had slain in fight.
Swift he bestrode his fire-fly steed;
  He bared his blade of the bent-grass blue;
He drove his spurs of the cockle-seed,
  And away like a glance of thought he flew,
To skim the heavens, and follow far
The fiery trail of the rocket-star.

Joseph Rodman Drake

THE OWL AND THE PUSSY-CAT

The Owl and the Pussy-Cat went to sea
    In a beautiful pea-green boat:
They took some honey, and plenty of money
    Wrapped up in a five-pound note.
The Owl looked up to the stars above,
    And sang to a small guitar,
"O lovely Pussy, O Pussy, my love,
    What a beautiful Pussy you are,
        You are,
        You are!
What a beautiful Pussy you are!"

Pussy said to the Owl, "You elegant fowl,
    How charmingly sweet you sing!
Oh! let us be married; too long we have tarried:
    But what shall we do for a ring?"
They sailed away, for a year and a day,
    To the land where the bong-tree grows;
And there in a wood a Piggy-wig stood,
    With a ring at the end of his nose,
        His nose,
        His nose,
With a ring at the end of his nose.

Dear Pig, are you willing to sell for one shilling
    Your ring?" Said the Piggy, "I will."
So they took it away, and were married next day
    By the Turkey who lives on the hill.
They dined on mince and slices of quince,
    Which they ate with a runcible spoon;
And hand in hand, on the edge of the sand,
    They danced by the light of the moon,
        The moon,
        The moon,
They danced by the light of the moon.

Edward Lear

GOOD HOTDOGS

For Kiki

Fifty cents apiece
To eat our lunch
We'd run
Straight from school
Instead of home
Two blocks
Then the store
That smelled like steam
You ordered
Because you had the money
Two hotdogs and two pops for here
Everything on the hotdogs
Except pickle lily
Dash those hotdogs
Into buns and splash on
All that good stuff

Yellow mustard and onions
And french fries piled on top all
Rolled up in a piece of wax
Paper for us to hold hot
In our hands
Quarters on the counter
Sit down
Good hotdogs
We'd eat
Fast till there was nothing left
But salt and poppy seeds even
The little burnt tips
Of french fries
We'd eat
you humming
And me swinging my legs

Sandra Cisneros

110

THE RED
WHEELBARROW

so much depends
upon

a red wheel
barrow

glazed with rain
water

beside the white
chickens.

William Carlos Williams

AFTERNOON ON A HILL

I will be the gladdest thing
   Under the sun!
I will touch a hundred flowers
   And not pick one.

I will look at cliffs and clouds
   With quiet eyes,
Watch the wind bow down the grass,
   And the grass rise.

And when lights begin to show
   Up from the town,
I will mark which must be mine,
   And then start down!

Edna St. Vincent Millay

GOBLIN FEET

I am off down the road
Where the fairy lanterns glowed
And the little pretty flitter-mice are flying:
A slender band of gray
It runs creepily away
And the hedges and the grasses are a-sighing.
The air is full of wings,
And of blundery beetle-things
That warn you with their whirring and their humming.
O! I hear the tiny horns
Of enchanted leprechauns
And the padded feet of many gnomes a-coming!

O! the lights! O! the gleams! O! the little tinkly sounds!
O! the rustle of their noiseless little robes!
O! the echo of their feet—of their happy little feet!
O! their swinging lamps in little starlit globes.

I must follow in their train
Down the crooked fairy lane
Where the coney-rabbits long ago have gone,
And where silvery they sing
On a moving moonlit ring
All a-twinkle with the jewels they have on.

They are fading round the turn
Where the glow-worms palely burn
And the echo of their padding feet is dying!
O! it's knocking at my heart—
Let me go! O! let me start!
For the little magic hours are all a-flying.

O! the warmth! O! the hum! O! the colors in the dark!
O! the gauzy wings of golden honey-flies!
O! the music of their feet—of their dancing goblin feet!
O! the magic! O! the sorrow when it dies.

J.R.R. Tolkien

THE SONG OF WANDERING AENGUS

I went out to the hazel wood,
Because a fire was in my head,
And cut and peeled a hazel wand,
And hooked a berry to a thread;
And when white moths were on the wing,
And moth-like stars were flickering out,
I dropped the berry in a stream
And caught a little silver trout.

When I had laid it on the floor
I went to blow the fire aflame,
But something rustled on the floor,
And some one called me by my name:
It had become a glimmering girl
With apple blossom in her hair
Who called me by my name and ran
And faded through the brightening air.

Though I am old with wandering
Through hollow lands and hilly lands,
I will find out where she has gone,
And kiss her lips and take her hands;
And walk among long dappled grass,
And pluck till time and times are done
The silver apples of the moon,
The golden apples of the sun.

William Butler Yeats

SCAFFOLDING

Masons, when they start upon a building,
Are careful to test out the scaffolding;

Make sure that planks won't slip at busy points,
Secure all ladders, tighten bolted joints.

And yet all this comes down when the job's done,
Showing off walls of sure and solid stone.

So if, my dear, there sometimes seems to be
Old bridges breaking between you and me,

Never fear. We may let the scaffolds fall,
Confident that we have built our wall.

Seamus Heaney

117

FROM SONG OF THE OPEN ROAD

Afoot and light-hearted, I take to the open road,
Healthy, free, the world before me,
The long brown path before me leading wherever I choose.

Henceforth I ask not good-fortune, I myself am good fortune,
Henceforth I whimper no more, postpone no more, need nothing,
Done with indoor complaints, libraries, querulous criticisms,
Strong and content, I travel the open road.

The earth, that is sufficient,
I do not want the constellations any nearer,
I know they are very well where they are,
I know they suffice for those who belong to them.

(Still here I carry my old delicious burdens,
I carry them, men and women, I carry them with me wherever I go,
I swear it is impossible for me to get rid of them,
I am fill'd with them, and I will fill them in return.)

Walt Whitman

THE RIDER

A boy told me
if he roller-skated fast enough
his loneliness couldn't catch up to him,

the best reason I ever heard
for trying to be a champion.

What I wonder tonight
pedaling hard down King William Street
is if it translates to bicycles.

A victory! To leave your loneliness
panting behind you on some street corner
while you float free into a cloud of sudden azaleas,
pink petals that have never felt loneliness,
no matter how slowly they fell.

Naomi Shihab Nye

"DO NOT BE AFRAID OF NO"

"Do not be afraid of no,
Who has so far so very far to go":

New caution to occur
To one who's inner scream set her to cede, for softer lapping
     and smooth fur!

Whose esoteric need
Was merely to avoid the nettle, to not-bleed.

Stupid, like a street
That beats into a dead end and dies there, with nothing left to
     reprimand or meet.

And like a candle fixed
Against dismay and countershine of mixed

Wild moon and sun. And like
A flying furniture, or bird with lattice wing; or gaunt thing,
    a-stammer down a nightmare neon peopled with condor,
    hawk and shrike.

To say yes is to die
A lot or a little. The dead wear capably their wry

Enameled emblems. They smell.
But that and that they do not altogether yell is all that we
    know well.

It is brave to be involved,
To be not fearful to be unresolved.

Her new wish was to smile
When answers took no airships, walked a while.

Gwendolyn Brooks

WHEN I HEARD THE LEARN'D ASTRONOMER

When I heard the learn'd astronomer,
When the proofs, the figures, were ranged in columns before me,
When I was shown the charts and diagrams, to add, divide, and measure them,
When I sitting heard the astronomer where he lectured with much applause in
the lecture-room,
How soon unaccountable I became tired and sick,
Till rising and gliding out I wander'd off by myself,
In the mystical moist night-air, and from time to time,
Look'd up in perfect silence at the stars.

Walt Whitman

HARLEM NIGHT SONG

Come,
Let us roam the night together
Singing.

I love you.

Across
The Harlem roof-tops
Moon is shining.
Night sky is blue.
Stars are great drops
Of golden dew.

Down the street
A band is playing.

I love you.

Come,
Let us roam the night together
Singing.

Langston Hughes

When I was young, I never understood why adults thought it was so important for children to go to bed. I suspected that it was mostly because they wanted to get some sleep themselves. And when I grew up, I discovered I was right! I hated going to bed early, especially in summer when I could hear my older cousins playing flashlight tag outside. Robert Louis Stevenson's poem "Bed in Summer" captures this feeling perfectly.

When they were very little, my children didn't like to go to bed either. One of their favorite books to read at bedtime was *The Bed Book*, by Sylvia Plath. It describes a nighttime of fantastic adventures, which they find much more appealing than soothing poems about falling asleep.

Still, bedtime can be a special time for reading together quietly and talking about things that happened during the busy day. The stories and poems we read at bedtime are often the ones we remember best when we grow up. I have also discovered that if you are one of those children who hates going to bed, sometimes if you ask your parents to read you a poem, they may let you stay up just a little bit later.

BEDTIME

BED IN SUMMER

In winter I get up at night
And dress by yellow candle-light.
In summer, quite the other way,
I have to go to bed by day.

I have to go to bed and see
The birds still hopping on the tree,
Or hear the grown-up people's feet
Still going past me in the street.

And does it not seem hard to you,
When all the sky is clear and blue,
And I should like so much to play,
To have to go to bed by day?

Robert Louis Stevenson

"SWEET AND LOW"

Sweet and low, sweet and low,
  Wind of the western sea,
Low, low, breathe and blow,
  Wind of the western sea!
  Over the rolling waters go,
  Come from the dying moon, and blow,
  Blow him again to me;
While my little one, while my pretty one sleeps.

Sleep and rest, sleep and rest,
  Father will come to thee soon;
Rest, rest, on mother's breast,
  Father will come to thee soon;
  Father will come to his babe in the nest,
  Silver sails all out of the west
  Under the silver moon:
Sleep, my little one, sleep, my pretty one, sleep.

Alfred, Lord Tennyson

128

SILVER

Slowly, silently, now the moon
Walks the night in her silver shoon;
This way, and that, she peers, and sees
Silver fruit upon silver trees;
One by one the casements catch
Her beams beneath the silvery thatch;
Couched in his kennel, like a log,
With paws of silver sleeps the dog;
From their shadowy cote the white breasts peep
Of doves in silver-feathered sleep;
A harvest mouse goes scampering by,
With silver claws, and silver eye;
And moveless fish in the water gleam,
By silver reeds in a silver stream.

Walter de la Mare

IF YOU'LL ONLY
GO TO SLEEP

The crimson rose
plucked yesterday,
the fire and cinnamon
of the carnation,

the bread I baked
with anise seed and honey,
and the goldfish
flaming in its bowl.

All these are yours,
baby born of woman,
if you'll only
go to sleep.

A rose, I say!
And a carnation!
Fruit, I say!
And honey!

And a sequined goldfish,
and still more I'll give you
if you'll only sleep
till morning.

Gabriela Mistral

FROM THE BED BOOK

Most Beds are Beds
For sleeping or resting,
But the *best* Beds are much
More interesting!

Not just a white little
Tucked-in-tight little
Nighty-night little
Turn-out-the-light little
      Bed—

        Instead
A Bed for Fishing
A Bed for Cats,
A Bed for a Troupe of
        Acrobats.

The *right* sort of Bed
(If you see what I mean)
Is a Bed that might
Be a Submarine

Nosing through water
Clear and green,
Silver and glittery
As a sardine.

Or a Jet-Propelled Bed
For Visiting Mars
With mosquito nest
For the shooting stars. . . .

Sylvia Plath

THE PLUMPUPPETS

When little heads weary have gone to their bed,
When all the good nights and prayers have been said,
Of all the good fairies that send bairns to rest
The little Plumpuppets are those I love best.

If your pillow is lumpy, or hot, thin, and flat,
The little Plumpuppets know just what they're at:
They plump up the pillow, all soft, cool and fat—
The little plumpuppets plump-up it!

The little Plumpuppets are fairies of beds;
They have nothing to do but watch sleepyheads;
They turn down the sheets and they tuck you in tight,
And dance on your pillow to wish you good night!

Christopher Morley

DREAM VARIATIONS

To fling my arms wide
In some place of the sun,
To whirl and to dance
Till the white day is done.
Then rest at cool evening
Beneath a tall tree
While night comes on gently,
    Dark like me—
That is my dream!

To fling my arms wide
In the face of the sun,
Dance! Whirl! Whirl!
Till the quick day is done.
Rest at pale evening . . .
A tall, slim tree . . .
Night coming tenderly
    Black like me.

Langston Hughes

133

THE MOON

There is such loneliness in that gold.
The moon of the nights is not the moon
Whom the first Adam saw. The long centuries
Of human vigil have filled her
With ancient lament. Look at her. She is your mirror.

Jorge Luis Borges

FROM IMAGINE ANGELS

<pre>
        IN   THIS
      IONS   MIR
    FLECT   ROR
    RE   I
    THE   AM
    LIKE   EN
    NOT   CLOSED
    AND   A
    GELS   LIVE
    AN   AND
    GINE   REAL
    MA   AS
      I   YOU
</pre>

Guillaume Apollinaire

KEEP A POEM IN YOUR POCKET

Keep a poem in your pocket
and a picture in your head
and you'll never feel lonely
at night when you're in bed.

The little poem will sing to you
the little picture bring to you
a dozen dreams to dance to you
at night when you're in bed.

So—
Keep a picture in your pocket
and a poem in your head
and you'll never feel lonely
at night when you're in bed.

Beatrice Schenk de Regniers

THE HOUSE WAS QUIET AND THE WORLD WAS CALM

The house was quiet and the world was calm.
The reader became the book; and summer night

Was like the conscious being of the book.
The house was quiet and the world was calm.

The words were spoken as if there was no book,
Except that the reader leaned above the page,

Wanted to lean, wanted much most to be
The scholar to whom his book is true, to whom

The summer night is like a perfection of thought.
The house was quiet because it had to be.

The quiet was part of the meaning, part of the mind:
The access of perfection to the page.

And the world was calm. The truth in a calm world,
In which there is no other meaning, itself

Is calm, itself is summer and night, itself
Is the reader leaning late and reading there.

Wallace Stevens

FOREIGN POEMS IN THEIR ORIGINAL LANGUAGES

PAGE 21:
¡MI CORAZÓN SE HA DORMIDO?
Antonio Machado

¡Mi corazón se ha dormido?
Colmenares de mis sueños
¿ya no labráis? ¿Está seca
la noria del pensamiento,
Los cangilones vacíos,
girando, de sombra llenos?
No, mi corazón no duerme.
Está despierto, despierto.
Ni duerme ni sueña, mira,
los claros ojos abiertos,
señas lejanas y escucha
a orillas del gran silencio.

PAGE 43:
PFAUUENFEDER
Rainer Maria Rilke

Pfauuenfeder:
in deiner Feinheit sondergleichen,
wie liebte ich dich schon als Kind.
Ich hielt dich für ein Liebeszeichen,
das sich an silberstillen Teichen
in kühler Nacht die Elfen reichen,
wenn alle Kinder schlafen sind.

Und weil Grossmütterchen, das gute,
mir oft von Wünschegerten las,
so träumte ich, du zartgemute,
in deinen feinen Fasern flute
die kluge Kraft der Rätselrute—
und suchte dich im Sommergras.

PAGE 43:
YŎNG É
Luo Binwang

é é é
Qū xiàng xiàng tiān gē
Bái máo fú lǘ shuǐ
Hóng zhǎng bō qīng bō

鵝鵝鵝
曲項向天歌
白毛浮綠水
紅掌撥清波

PAGE 46:
FURUIKE YA
Basho

Furuike ya
kawazu tobikomu
Mizu no oto

牡丹藥 深く分け出づる蜂の名残かな

PAGE 46:
BOTAN SHIBE FUKAKU
Basho

Botan shibe fukaku
Wakeizuru hachi no
Nagori ka na

古池や 蛙飛び込む水の音

PAGE 81:
ODA A LOS CALCETINES
Pablo Neruda

Me trajo Maru Mori
un par
de calcetines
que tejió con sus manos
de pastora,
dos calcetines suaves
como liebres.
En ellos
metí los pies
como en
dos
estuches
tejidos
con hebras del
crepúsculo
y pellejo de ovejas.
Violentos calcetines,
mis pies fueron
dos pescados
de lana,
dos largos tiburones

de azul ultramarino
atravesados
por una trenza de oro,
dos gigantescos mirlos,
dos canoñes:
mis pies
fueron honrados
de este modo
por
estos
celestiales
calcetines.
Eran
tan hermosos
que por primera vez
mis pies me parecieron
inaceptables
como dos decrépitos
bomberos, bomberos
indignos
de aquel fuego
bordado,
de aquellos luminosos
calcetines.

PAGE 97:
CARACOLA
A Natalia Jiménez
Federico García Lorca

Me han traído una caracola.

Dentro le canta
un mar de mapa.
Mi corazón
se llena de agua
con pececillos
de sombra y plata.

Me han traído una caracola.

PAGE 130:
CON TAL QUE DUERMAS
Gabriela Mistral

La rosa colorada
cogida ayer;

el fuego y la canela
que llaman clavel;

el pan horneado
de anís con miel,
y el pez de la redoma
que la hace arder:
todito tuyo
hijito de mujer,
con tal que quieras
dormirte de una vez.

La rosa, digo:
digo el clavel.
La fruta, digo,
y digo que la miel;

y el pez de luces
y más y más también,
¡con tal que duermas
hasta el amanecer!

PAGE 134:
LA LUNA
A Maria Kodama
Jorge Luis Borges

Hay tanta soledad en ese oro.
La luna de las noches no es la luna
Que vio el primer Adán. Los largos siglos
De la vigilia humana la han colmado
De antiguo llanto. Mirala. Es tu espejo.

PAGE 134:
FROM COEUR COURONNE ET MIROIR
Guillaume Apollinaire

```
              DANS
        FLETS        CE
     RE                  MI
   LES                     ROIR
 SONT                        JE
 ME                          SUIS
 COM                          EN
 NON                          CLOS
  ET                          VI
  GES                        VANT
   AN                        ET
   LES                      VRAI
    NE                     COM
     GI                   ME
      MA              ON
              I
```

INDEX OF FIRST LINES

ACKNOWLEDGMENTS

Guillaume Apollinaire, "Imagine Angels," translated by Kenneth Koch, from *Rose, Where Did You Get That Red?: Teaching Poetry to Children*. Copyright © 1973 by Kenneth Koch. Reprinted with the permission of Random House, Inc.

Basho, "An old silent pond . . ." and "Farewell! Like a bee" from *Cricket Songs: Japanese Haiku*, translated by Harry Behn. Copyright © 1964 by Harry Behn and renewed 1992 by Prescott Behn, Pamela Behn Adam, and Peter Behn. Reprinted with the permission of Marian Reiner.

Hilaire Belloc, "The Frog" and "The Early Morning." Copyright © 1970 The Estate of Hilaire Belloc. Reprinted with the permission of PFD on behalf of The Estate of Hilaire Belloc.

Elizabeth Bishop, "The Fish" from *The Complete Poems 1926–1979*. Copyright © 1965 by Elizabeth Bishop. Copyright ©1979, 1983 by Alice Helen Methfessel. Reprinted with the permission of Farrar, Straus & Giroux, Inc.

Jorge Luis Borges, "The Moon," translated by Willis Barnstone. Reprinted with the permission of the translator.

Jacqueline Bouvier, "Thoughts" and "Sea Joy." Reprinted with the permission of The Estate of Jacqueline Kennedy Onassis.

Joseph Brodsky, "To a Fellow Poet" from *Collected Poems in English*. Copyright © 2000 by the Estate of Joseph Brodsky. Reprinted with the permission of Farrar, Straus & Giroux, LLC.

Gwendolyn Brooks, "do not be afraid of no" from *Annie Allen*. Copyright 1949 by Gwendolyn Brooks. Reprinted with the permission of the Estate of Gwendolyn Brooks.

Sandra Cisneros, "Good Hotdogs" from *My Wicked Wicked Ways* (New York: Alfred A. Knopf, 1989). Copyright © 1989 by Sandra Cisneros. Reprinted with the permission of Susan Bergholz Literary Services, New York. All rights reserved.

E. E. Cummings, "in Just-" "little tree," and "maggie and milly and molly and may" from *Complete Poems 1904–1962*, edited by George J. Firmage. Copyright 1923, 1925, 1951, 1953, © 1956, 1984, 1991 by the Trustees for the E. E. Cummings Trust. Copyright © 1976 by George James Firmage. Reprinted with the permission of Liveright Publishing Corporation.

Walter de la Mare, "Me" from *The Complete Poems of Walter de la Mare*. Reprinted with the permission of The Literary Trustees of Walter de la Mare and The Society of Authors as their representative.

Emily Dickinson, "'Hope' is the thing with Feathers" and "These are the days when Birds come back" from *The Poems of Emily Dickinson*, edited by Thomas H. Johnson. Copyright 1951, © 1955, 1979 by the President and Fellows of Harvard College. Reprinted with the permission of the publishers and the Trustees of Amherst College.

T. S. Eliot, "Mr. Mistoffelees" from *Old Possum's Book of Practical Cats*. Copyright 1939 by T. S. Eliot, renewed © 1967 by Esme Valerie Eliot. Reprinted with the permission of Harcourt, Inc., and Faber and Faber Ltd.

Rachel Field, "Something Told the Wild Geese" from *Poems*. Copyright 1934 by Macmillan Publishing Company, renewed © 1965 by Arthur S. Pederson. Reprinted with the permission of Simon & Schuster Books for Young Readers, an imprint of Simon & Schuster Children's Publishing Division.

Robert Frost, "Fireflies in the Garden," "The Last Word of a Bluebird," "The Pasture," "Stopping by Woods on a Snowy Evening," and "The Road Not Taken," from *The Poetry of Robert Frost*, edited by Edward Connery Lathem. Copyright 1942, 1951, 8 1956, 1961, 1962 by Robert Frost, © by Lesley Frost Ballantine, 1923, 1928, 1949, © 1969 by Henry Holt and Company. Reprinted with the permission of Henry Holt and Company, LLC.

Nikki Giovanni, "The Reason I Like Chocolate" from *Vacation Time*. Copyright © 1980 by Nikki Giovanni. Reprinted with the permission of HarperCollins Publishers, Inc.

Thomas Hardy, "Snow in the Suburbs" from *The Complete Poems of Thomas Hardy*, edited by James Gibson. Copyright 1925 by Macmillan Publishing Company, renewed 1953 by Lloyds Bank Ltd. Reprinted with the permission of Macmillan Publishing Company and Macmillan Press, Ltd.

Seamus Heaney, "Scaffolding" from *Death of a Naturalist*. Copyright ©1969 by Seamus Heaney. Reprinted with the permission of Farrar, Straus & Giroux, LLC and Faber & Faber, Ltd.

A. E. Housman, "Amelia Mixed the Mustard" from *The Collected Poems of A. E. Housman*. Copyright 1939, 1940 by Henry Holt and Company, renewed © 1967 by Robert E. Symons. Reprinted with the permission of The Society of Authors as literary representative of the Estate of A. E. Housman.

Langston Hughes, "Dream Variations," "Harlem Night Song," and "April Rain Song" from *The Collected Poems of Langston Hughes*. Copyright © 1994 by The Estate of Langston Hughes. Reprinted with the permission of Alfred A. Knopf, a division of Random House, Inc.

Ted Hughes, "Roger the Dog" from *What is the Truth?* Copyright © 1984, 1995 by Ted Hughes. Reprinted with the permission of Faber & Faber, Ltd.

Galway Kinnell, "Saint Francis and the Sow" from *Mortal Acts, Mortal Words*. Copyright © 1980 by Galway Kinnell. Reprinted with the permission of Houghton Mifflin Company. All rights reserved.

Vachel Lindsay, "The Little Turtle" from *Collected Poems, Revised Edition* (New York: Macmillan, 1925). Originally collected in *The Golden Whales of California and Other Rhymes in the American Language* (New York: Macmillan, 1920), p. 104.

Federico García Lorca, "Seashell," translated by Alan S. Trueblood, from *Collected Poems, Revised Bilingual Edition*, edited by Christopher Maurer. Copyright © 1989, 1990, 1991, and 2001 by Catherine Brown, William Bryant Logan, Alan S. Trueblood, and Christopher Maurer. Reprinted with the permission of Farrar, Straus & Giroux, LLC.

Antonio Machado, "Has My Heart Gone to Sleep?" translated by Alan S. Trueblood, from *Selected Poems*. Copyright © 1983 by the President and Fellows of Harvard College. Reprinted with the permission of Harvard University Press.

*For Jack—I thought of you the whole time I was putting
this book together and I hope you always love poetry.*
— CK

*With love and endless gratitude to Allen Spiegel, a great teacher
for over thirty years. And to all stouthearted, encouraging teachers
and librarians everywhere—thank you.*
— JJM

Acknowledgments:

*I would like to thank Greer Baxter for contributing her enthusiasm, critical insight,
and wonderful mother to this project. I would also like to thank two of the most
inspiring teachers I have ever met, Susan Sagor and Barbara Berresford, for their
suggestions, and for instilling a love of poetry in generations of students, including
contributors to our family's Poetry Scrapbook.*

— CK

*Thanks to my wife Bonnie for her patience and love, my son Nikolai and my daughter
Adelaine for their open-hearted enthusiasm—for being my family.*

— JJM

Introductions and collection copyright © 2005 by Caroline Kennedy
Paintings copyright © 2005 by Jon J Muth
Front cover photograph copyright © by Caroline Kennedy

For further acknowledgments, see page 142.

1 3 5 7 9 10 8 6 4 2

This book is set in 12-point Goudy.
Hand lettering by Leah Palmer Preiss

Book Designer: Roberta Pressel
Production Director: Linda Prather
Copy Chief: Monica Mayper
Managing Editor: Jaime Herbeck

Reinforced binding

ISBN 0-7868-5111-2

Library of Congress Cataloging-in-Publication Data on file.

Visit www.hyperionbooksforchildren.com